A Circle of Cats

Charles de Lint

Illustrated by **Charles Vess**

VIKING

VIKING

Published by Penguin Group

Penguin Group (USA), Inc., 345 Hudson Street, New York, New York 10014, U.S.A.

Penguin Books Ltd, 80 Strand, London WC2R 0RL, England

Penguin Books Australia Ltd, 250 Camberwell Road, Camberwell, Victoria 3124, Australia

Penguin Books Canada Ltd, 10 Alcorn Avenue, Toronto, Ontario, Canada M4V 3B2

Penguin Books (N.Z.) Ltd, 182-190 Wairau Road, Auckland 10, New Zealand

First published in 2003 by Viking, a division of Penguin Young Readers Group.

Text copyright © Charles de Lint, 2003
Illustrations copyright © Charles Vess, 2003
All rights reserved

1 3 5 7 9 10 8 6 4 2

LIBRARY OF CONGRESS CATALOGING-IN-PUBLICATION DATA IS AVAILABLE.
ISBN 0-670-03647-1

Manufactured in China
Set in Deepdene
Book design by Nancy Brennan

For my two best gals, MaryAnn and Clare—C.d.L.

For June who was "there" in the beginning, and for Miso, my cat—
she always liked to climb up high.—C.V.

ONCE THERE WAS A FOREST OF HICKORY AND BEECH, sprucey-pine, birch and oak. It started at the edge of a farmer's pasture and seemed to go on forever, up hill and down. There were a few abandoned homesteads to be found in its reaches, overgrown and uninhabitable now, and deep in a hidden clearing there was a beech tree so old that only the hills themselves remembered the days when it was a sapling. Above that old grandfather tree, the forest marched up to the hilltops in ever denser thickets of rhododendrons and brush until nothing stood between the trees and stars. Below it, a creek ran along the bottom of a dark narrow valley, no more than a trickle in some places, wider in others. Occasionally the water tumbled down rough staircases of stone and rounded rocks.

On a quiet day, when the wind was still, the creek could be heard all the way up to where the old beech stood. Under its branches, cats would come to dream and be dreamed. Black cats and calicos, white cats and marmalade ones, too. But they hadn't yet gathered on the day the orphan girl fell asleep among its roots, nestling in the weeds and long grass like the gangly, tousle-haired girl she was.

Her name was Lillian.

She hadn't meant to fall asleep, but she was a bit like a cat herself, forever wandering in the woods, chasing after squirrels and rabbits as fast as her skinny legs could take her when the

fancy struck, climbing trees like a possum, able to doze in the sun at a moment's notice. And sometimes with no notice at all.

This morning she'd been hunting fairies down by the creek where it pooled wide for a spell. The only way you could cross it here was by the stepping stones laid out in an irregular pattern from one bank to the other.

She never found fairies, no matter how hard she looked, though some days she could feel them in the air around her, tiny invisible presences as quick as dragonflies. The air would hum with the rapid beat of their wings, but no matter how quickly she turned and spun, they were never there when she looked.

She and Aunt lived miles from anyone, deep in the hills, halfway down the slope between an abandoned apple orchard and the creek. It seemed the perfect place to find fairies if ever there was one, and if the stories the old folks told were true. But no matter how quietly Lillian prowled through the woods, no matter how often she crept up on a mushroom fairy ring, the little people were never there.

"Don't you go troubling the spirits," Aunt told her on more than one occasion. "They were here before us and they'll still be here when we're gone. Best you just leave them be."

"But why?"

"Because they're not partial to being bothered by some little red-haired girl who's got nothing better to do than stick her nose in other folks' business. When it comes to spirits, it's best not to bring yourself to their attention. Elsewise you never know what you might be calling down on yourself."

But that was hard advice for a twelve-year-old girl.

"I'm not troubling anyone," she would tell the oldest apple tree in the orchard, lying on the ground, looking up into its leaves. "I just want to say hello hello."

But it was hard to say hello to fairies she couldn't find.

That morning she'd done her chores as she did every morning. She fed the chickens, throwing an extra handful of grain

into the grass for the sparrows and other small birds that wait-
ed for the promise of her bounty in the branches of the wild
rosebushes that grew nearby. She milked their one cow, setting
out a saucer for the stray cats that would come out of the forest
while she put the cow out to pasture and brought the milk in to
Aunt. After a breakfast of biscuits and honeyed tea, she weeded
the vegetable patch, and then the rest of the day was hers to do
what she wanted.

She set off on a ramble, running up the hill to leave a piece of one of her breakfast biscuits under the boughs of the Apple Tree Man.

That's what Aunt called the oldest apple tree in their orchard gone wild. He stood near the very top of the hill, over-looking the meadow dotted with wildflowers and beehives and the other apple trees.

"Why do you call him that?" Lillian had asked the first time she'd heard his name. "Is there a real man living in the tree?"

He'd be a gnarled, twisty sort of a man, she thought, to live in that old twisty tree. She probably daydreamed as much about him as she did about fairies, especially when she was lying under his branches.

"I don't know the why or where of it," Aunt replied. "But that's what we've always called the oldest apple tree. Only we didn't leave out food for him like you do." She shook her head. "You're just feeding the raccoons and squirrels."

Lillian didn't think so, not at all. There was an Apple Tree Man, just like there were fairies. He was shy, that was all. Private.

So, with her chores done, breakfast finished, and the Apple Tree Man fed, she went down into the hollow. She wandered upstream from the stepping stones to where the creek tumbled down a staircase of rocks, enjoying the change of temperature on

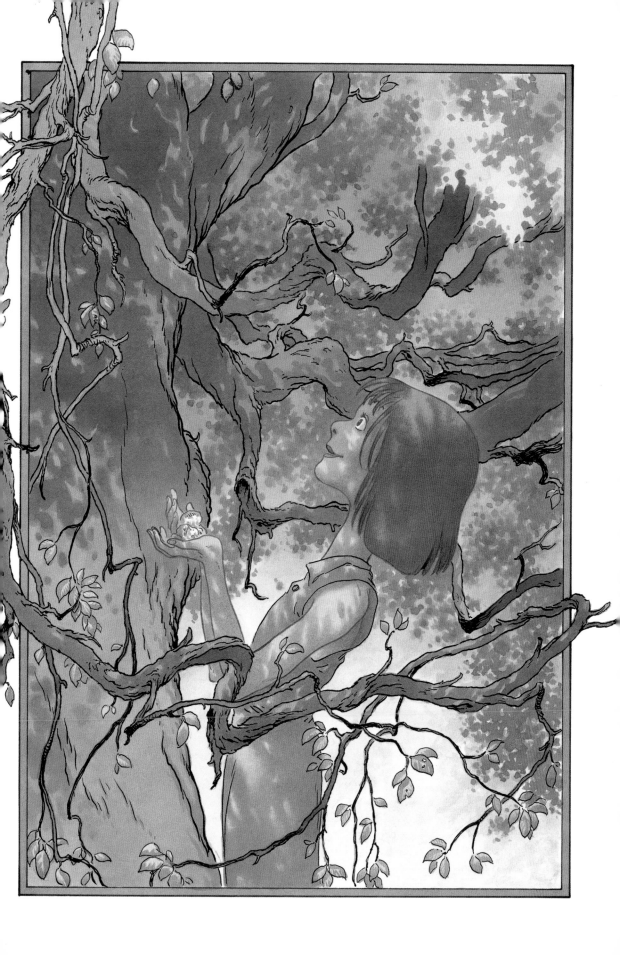

her arms when she walked from sunlight into shadow and then out again. At the waterfall, she poked with a stick at the pebbles shiny under water, balancing on the slick rocks and lichen until she felt the weight of someone's attention upon her. Looking up, she found herself face to face with a handsome, white-tailed deer. He stood on the edge of a tangle of rhododendrons, with the sprucey-pines and yellow birch rising up the hillside behind him.

Deer were almost as good as fairies, so far as Lillian was concerned.

"Hello hello, you," she said.

When he turned and bolted, she ran in pursuit. Not to catch him, not to scare him. Just for the fun of seeing how fast they both could run.

They ran up hill and down. They ran through thickets of hickory and yellow birch, across sudden meadows where the grass and weeds slapped against their legs, up rock-strewn slopes dusky with moss and ferns, back down into the hollow where the creek ran with them. They ran and ran, the deer bounding gracefully, Lillian scrambling and leaping, but no less quick for that.

Sometimes she could almost touch him. Sometimes all she could see of him was the flash of a white tail, but when he saw she was falling behind, he would pretend to catch his own breath, only to bolt away again as she drew near.

They ran through familiar fields and meadows and deep into parts of the forest where Lillian had never been before. The trees were older here and the thickets sometimes so dense that she had to wriggle under them while the deer bounded gracefully over.

That was how she finally found herself lying under that old

grandfather beech tree in its hidden clearing, the deer gone his own way while she collapsed in a tangle of limbs in the tall grass and fell asleep.

And that was where the snake bit her.

It was an awful, dreadful snake, like in that old song Aunt sometimes sang.

Lillian never even knew it was there under the tree with her until it struck.

The snake had been sleeping when Lillian curled up in the grass, all coiled up only inches from her foot. Dreaming, Lillian moved a leg suddenly, kicking at a milkweed head in her dream which, in turn, disturbed the snake's own drowsy nap. The bright pain from its first strike woke her, but by then it was already too late. It struck a second time, a third. She tried to rise, to call Aunt for help, but the venom stole her strength and dropped her back onto the ground, shivering and cold.

She knew she was dying, just like the little girl in the song.

The fog of pain already lay too thick for her to see the cats come out of the long grass. Some of them she would have known, because they came to visit her in the morning. Others were strangers, cats no one saw, they lived so deep in the forest; but they, too, knew of the skinny, half-wild girl who fed their cousins.

The one Lillian called Big Orange—almost the size of a bobcat, with the russet fur of a fox—was in the lead. He pounced on the snake and bit off its head, *snap*, just like that. Black Nessie batted the head away with a quick swipe of her paw. Two of the kittens jumped on the snake's thrashing body, growling and clawing and biting, but it was already in its death throes and couldn't harm anyone else now. The other cats gathered in their circle, only this time, instead of calling up cat dreams, they had a dying girl in the middle of them.

Lillian wasn't aware of any of this. She was falling up into a bright tunnel of light, which was an odd experience, because she'd never fallen up before. She hadn't even known it was possible.

She wasn't scared now, or even in pain. She just wished the voices she heard would stop talking, because they were holding her back. They wouldn't let her fall all the way up into the tunnel of light.

"We have to save her."

"We can't. It's too late."

"Unless . . ."

"Unless we change her into something that isn't dying."

"But Father said we must never again—"

"I'll accept the weight of Father's anger."

"We all will."

They turned their attention to Lillian and woke cat magic

under the boughs of their old beech tree. First they swayed back and forth, in time with each other. Then their voices lifted in a strange, scratchy harmony like a kitchen full of fiddles not quite in tune with each other, but not so out of tune as to be entirely unpleasant. A golden light rose up from their music to glow in the air between them. It hung there, pulsing to the rhythm of their song for a long moment, before it went from cat to cat in the circle, round and round.

Three times the light went around the circuit before it left them and came to rest on the dying girl in the middle of their circle. The cats lifted their heads. They could see the soul of the girl floating up through the boughs of the beech. Their scratchy song rose higher, and the light rose with it, chasing after the soul like a rope of golden light. When it finally caught up, the rope wrapped around her, pulling her soul back into her body.

The cats fell silent, staring at the rise and fall of Lillian's chest, and exchanged pleased looks with one another. But then, frightened by what they had done, by what Father might do when he found out, they retreated back into the forest.

Lillian woke up and had a long, lazy stretch. What an odd dream, she thought. She lifted a paw, licked it, and was starting to clean her face when she realized what she was doing. She held the paw in front of her face. It was definitely a paw, covered in fur and minus a thumb. Where was her hand?

She looked at the rest of herself and saw only a cat's calico body, as lean and lanky as her own, but covered in fur and certainly not the one she knew.

"What's become of me?" she said.

"You're a kitten," a voice said from above.

She looked up to find a squirrel looking down at her from a branch of the beech. It seemed to be laughing at her.

"I'm not a cat, I'm a girl," she told it.

"And I'm an old hound dog," the squirrel replied.

Then it made a passable imitation of a hound's mournful howl and bounded off, higher up into the tree.

"But I *am* a girl," Lillian said.

She started to get up, but she seemed to have too many legs and sprawled back onto the grass.

"Or at least I was."

She tried to get up again, moving gingerly until she realized that this cat's body she was in knew how to get about. Instead of worrying about how to get up and move, she had to let herself move naturally, the way she did when she was a girl.

This time when she stood she saw the body of the headless snake, and it all came back to her. She backed away, the hair rising all along her spine, her tail puffing out. It hadn't been a dream. She'd been snakebit. She'd been dying. And then . . . and then . . . what? She remembered a tunnel of light and voices.

Fairies, she thought. The fairies had come to rescue her.

"Squirrel!" she called up into the branches of the tree. "Did you see the fairies? Did you see them change me?"

There was no reply.

"I don't think I want to be a cat," she said.

Now she really had to find the fairies.

By the time she'd bounded all the way down to the creek, she was more comfortable in her new body, though no happier about being in it. There were no fairies about, but then there never were when she was looking for them. Whatever was she going to do? She couldn't go through the rest of her life as a cat.

Finding a quiet pool along the bank, she looked in. And here was the strangest thing of all. There was her own girl's face looking back at her from the water. When she lifted what was plainly a paw, the reflection lifted a hand.

Lillian sat back on her haunches to consider this.

"They changed you," a voice said from above. "Now you're not quite girl, not quite cat."

She looked up to see an old crow perched on a branch.

"But why?" she asked.

"You were dying. They had no madstone to draw the poison out, nor milk to soak it in, nor hands to do the work and hold the stone in place. So they did what they could. They changed you into something that's not dying."

Lillian had seen a madstone before. Harlene Welch, the midwife, had one. Her husband found it in the stomach of a deer he was field-dressing—a smooth, flat, grayish-looking stone about the size of a silver dollar. You had to soak it in milk and then lay it against the bite, where it would cling, only falling off when all the poison had been drawn out. It worked on bites from both snakes and rabid animals.

"Will I be like this forever?" Lillian asked.

"Maybe, maybe not," the crow said.

Lillian would have asked the crow more, but just then the belling sound of Aunt's big iron triangle came ringing down from the cabin. Suppertime. The crow flew off and Lillian jumped from stone to stone across the creek and ran up the hill.

"Now what have we here?" Aunt said as Lillian came running up to her.

"It's me, it's me!" she cried. "Lillian."

But unlike the squirrel and the crow, Aunt didn't hear words, only a plaintive meowing. She smiled and picked Lillian up, scratching her under her chin. Lillian couldn't help it. She immediately started to purr.

"Now where did you come from?" Aunt said. She looked off across the fields. "And where *is* that girl?"

"I'm here, I'm here," Lillian cried from her arms.

But Aunt still couldn't understand her. She brought her inside and gave her a saucer of milk, which Lillian immediately began to lap up because, after all, it was suppertime, and she was hungry from the long day's activities.

When she was done, she wove in and out between Aunt's legs, but while Aunt would bend down to pat her, she was plainly worried and stood at the doorway looking out at where the dusk was drawing long shadows across the hillside.

They had no phone. They had no close neighbors. So eventually Aunt took the lantern and went out looking for her niece.

She made her way down to the creek first, Lillian trailing after her, still a kitten rather than a girl. Aunt walked almost a mile up the hollow, her lantern light bobbing in the dark woods, then crossed over the creek and came back the other way. Lillian didn't follow. She already knew where she was, and if Aunt wasn't going to listen to her, there was nothing she could do.

"I want to be a girl again," she said into the darkness.

Something rustled in the tree above her. She looked up to see an owl peering down at her with his saucer eyes.

"Well, now," it said. "You should have thought of that before you let that snake bite you."

Why did everyone only talk to her from the branches of a tree? she thought.

"I didn't *let* it bite me," she said. "It just did. And besides, I didn't even know it was there."

"Ignorance is no excuse."

That was one of Aunt's favorite expressions.

"I don't want to be a cat anymore," she told the owl.

"I don't blame you."

"It's not that I don't like cats."

The owl made a hrumphing sound. "Just when I thought you were showing some common sense."

"It's that I'm supposed to be a girl," she went on.

"A snakebit, dying girl?"

"Well, no. I'd rather be alive and well. Would the fairies change me back, do you think?"

"Fairies?" the owl said. "It wasn't fairies that changed you. It was cats."

"Cats? But ..."

"Cats are magic, too."

Lillian supposed the owl was right. Didn't Aunt always say, if cats weren't the devil, then they were the devil's friend? And when the old people told stories, devils and fairies sometimes seemed interchangeable.

"Why would they do it?"

"To save your life, you foolish girl."

Of course.

"That was kind of them," Lillian said.

"Who knows what they had in mind," the owl told her.

"Perhaps if I asked them most politely they would change me back."

The owl shook his head slowly. "You could try, but they'll ask something of you for their help."

"What sort of something?"

"Only they can tell you that. But I know this: it will be something you hold dear. That's always the way of it."

Lillian sighed. "But they're the only ones that can change me back into a girl?"

"I suppose," the owl told her, not sounding so sure.

Lillian looked down the creek where she could still see the bobbing of Aunt's lantern. Could still hear Aunt's voice, calling for her. She wanted to go to Aunt, but what was the use? Aunt couldn't help her. No one could.

"I thought they were fairies," she said. "The ones that changed me. I've always wanted to see fairies."

"You only have to open your eyes," the owl told her.

Easy for you to say, she thought, with eyes so big.

"Is it so bad to be a cat?" the owl asked as she started to walk away. "Wouldn't it be better to be a living cat than a dead girl?"

But she only thanked the owl and went to find that old beech tree where the cats had worked their magic.

It was harder to do that she'd imagined it would be. She'd always had a good sense of direction and saw no reason why being a cat should change that, but every time she set out in what she was sure was the right direction, she ended up somewhere else instead. The third time she lost her way she found herself in the apple orchard near the cabin, completely on the wrong side of the creek.

If this was more cat magic, it wasn't very nice. It wasn't very nice at all.

If this kept up, she was going to be a cat forever and ever.

Slowly she trudged over to the Apple Tree Man's tree and sat down under its branches where she'd happily dreamed so many times before. She wanted to be brave, but she couldn't stop the little mewing sounds that started to come from her throat.

"What's the matter, little kitten?"

Lillian looked up into the boughs of the apple tree, but for once there was no one up there. Instead the voice had come from the other side of the tree, where she could make out the shape of a man sitting there on the slope, hidden in the shadows. A man who could understand her.

"I'm not a cat, I'm a girl," she said, and then she told him her story.

"I know you," the man said when she was done. "You're Lillian. Every morning you bring me my breakfast."

Lillian stood up and peered closer at the man.

"Who are you?" she asked.

"You call me the Apple Tree Man."

Now here was some real magic, Lillian thought, forgetting for the moment that she'd been changed from a girl into a kitten.

A man who lived in a tree.

"I think I can help you," he said. "I have a madstone in some old corner of my tree. Let me have a look."

Lillian watched open-mouthed as the shadowy figure of the man stood up and stepped into the tree. One moment he was there, just as gnarly and twisty as she'd imagined he'd be, and the next he was gone.

"Here you go," he said, stepping out of the tree again.

He offered her a small, smooth, flat stone that was as white as moonlight. When Lillian tried to take it from him, it slid right out of her mouth.

"Let me carry it for you," he said.

"But carry it where?" Lillian asked. "I don't even know how to find that cat-magicked tree."

"I know the way," he told her.

He put the madstone in his pocket, picked her up, and set off in what she was sure was the entirely wrong direction. But very quickly the dark forest, already changed by the shadows and moonlight, became more unfamiliar still. And then there was a smell in the air—a smell Lillian remembered from when she'd been in the old beech tree's clearing. It was the smell of cats, mysterious and wild, and the smell of something else, wilder and older and more secret still.

She was glad to have the Apple Tree Man's company as they approached the beech. It made her feel brave and strong. She was trotting along beside him now, still marveling that there really was a man living in the oldest tree of the orchard. And here he was helping her and everything.

But once they got to the beech tree, her bravery faltered.

"What … what should I do?" she asked.

"Call the cats," he told her.

So she did. She cleared her little cat throat and "Hello hello," she called. "Please don't be angry, cats, but I need your help again."

But it wasn't the cats that came in response to her call.

A branch creaked in the boughs above and then she thought she heard a rumbling from under the hill, as though old tree roots were shifting against stone. She gave the Apple Tree Man a worried look, but he wasn't looking at her. His attention was elsewhere. There was the faintest rustle in the grass from the other side of the tree, and then Lillian saw what he was looking at. A large black panther stepped into view, moving like a ghost in the shadows.

Lillian thought her heart would stop in its little cat chest.

"Who . . . ?" she began.

"Lillian," the Apple Tree Man said. "Meet the Father of Cats."

"Hello, cousin," the panther said. His dark gaze turned to her. "Hello, child."

His voice was a low growl, like an old bear woken from its sleep. When he lay down to look at her, he was still much taller than she was, his tail going *pat-pat-pat* on the ground behind him, the way a cat's will before it pounces.

"Why do you need my help?" he asked.

"Please, sir," Lillian said. "I want to be a girl again. And Aunt needs me, she does."

He cocked his head. "And what is it that you so dislike about the shape of a cat?"

"Oh, nothing. Honestly. But I'm a girl, you see, not a cat."

"What will you give me if I help you?"

The owl had warned her. This panther was probably the devil in disguise, and what he really wanted was her soul. Lillian looked to the Apple Tree Man for help, but he shook his head as if to say, this you must deal with on your own. She turned back to the panther.

"I don't think I have anything you would want," she said.

"What if I asked you to come away with me for a year and a day?"

Where to? Lillian thought. Down below?

"I . . . I don't think I could go," she told him. "I'd miss Aunt too much. And she'd be so sad. Listen to her calling for me down by the creek."

And it was true. If you turned your ear the right way, you could hear Aunt's voice coming up from where she still searched for Lillian.

"Mmm," the panther said. Then he, too, looked at the Apple Tree Man. "I've told my children not to work this magic, but they didn't listen. You see what problems it causes?"

"She would have died otherwise."

"Mmm."

"She means no harm," the Apple Tree Man added, "and has done only good. She always spares grain for the sparrows. She gives your children milk. She brings me a share of her breakfast every morning."

"Mmm," the panther said a third time.

It was a deep, rumbly sound. The sound of him thinking, Lillian realized.

"You've a madstone soaked in milk?" the panther finally asked. "For if I change her, she will need it."

"I have the stone," the Apple Tree Man said. "I can soak it in milk."

"Then do so."

The Apple Tree Man gave her a reassuring smile, then turned and left them, a strange moving figure with his gnarly, twisted limbs.

It was hard waiting for him to return. The whole of the night seemed to be holding its breath as Lillian listened to the continued *pat-pat-pat* of the panther's tail tapping the ground.

"They say one good turn deserves another," the panther finally said.

"Please, sir," Lillian said. "That's not why I shared our food and milk."

"I know. And that's why I will help you. But you will owe me a favor. I might ask it of you. I might ask it of your children, or your children's children. Will you accept the debt?"

Lillian had to gather her courage before she could answer.

"Only . . . only if no one will be hurt by it," she said.

The panther gave her a grave nod. "That's a good answer," he said. "Now here comes our apple tree friend. Lie down and we will see how we may help you."

Lillian did as she was told. The last things she saw before she closed her eyes were the Apple Tree Man carrying a tin mug, and the deep golden glow that started up in the panther's yellow eyes. The last things she heard were the faint sound of Aunt's voice in the distance, and the low rumbling music of the panther's song as he called up his magic. Then there was a flare of pain such as she'd only felt once before, when the snake bit her. It lasted only a moment, but it felt like forever before the cool, milk-wet stone was laid against the bites and she drifted away.

When she woke again, she and the Apple Tree Man were alone under the beech tree. But she was a girl once more. She sat up, hugging herself, and grinned at him.

"I'm me again," she said.

He smiled. "You were always you. Now you just look more familiar, that's all." He hesitated, then added, "The Father of Cats said he had one word for you and it was 'remember.' Do you understand what he meant?"

Lillian nodded. "It's the payment I owe him. I have to always carry a debt, never knowing when he might ask for it to be paid. And he said, if I don't pay it, then the debt will carry on to my children, or my children's children."

"Does that trouble you?"

Lillian thought about it.

"I don't think so. I made him promise that I'd only help if no one was to be hurt by my help."

The Apple Tree Man smiled. "That was wise of you."

"Do you think he's the devil?" Lillian asked.

That made her companion laugh. "Hardly. The Father of Cats was here before there was such a word as 'devil.'"

"Oh."

She looked at him with his wrinkly face and his gnarly limbs. She remembered him stepping into the tree and then back out again with the white madstone in his twisty fingers.

"And are you a fairy man?" she had to ask.

He shook his head. "I'm only what you see. The old spirit of an old tree." He looked up into the branches of the beech. "Though not so old as this grandfather."

He stood up and took her hand. "Come," he said. "We should go."

"I would like to see the fairies sometime," Lillian said after they'd been walking for a few minutes.

She didn't remember crossing the creek, but suddenly, here they were in familiar fields with the orchard nearby.

The Apple Tree Man laughed. "You have only to open your eyes," he said, echoing what the owl had told her earlier.

"But I do. I run here and there and everywhere with my eyes wide open but I never see anything. Fairy-like, I mean."

He sat down and she sat beside him.

"Try looking from the corner of your eye," he said. He lifted a hand and pointed down the hill. "What do you see there?"

She saw the bobbing of Aunt's lantern as she returned from her fruitless search. She saw dark fields, dotted with apple trees and old beehives. She didn't see even one fairy.

"Give it a sidelong glance," the Apple Tree Man told her.

So she turned her head and looked at the bob of Aunt's lantern from the corner of her eye.

"I still don't see . . ."

Anything, she was going to say. But it wasn't true. The slope was now filled with small, dancing lights, flickering like fire-flies. Only these weren't magical bugs—they were magical people. Tiny glowing people with dragonfly wings, who swooped and spun through the air, leaving behind a trail of laughter and snatches of song.

"Oh, thank you for showing them to me," Lillian said, turning back to her companion.

But the Apple Tree Man was gone.

Lillian reached forward and touched where he'd been sitting.

"Good-bye good-bye," she said softly. "Tomorrow I'll bring you a whole plate of biscuits for your breakfast."

Then she jumped to her feet and ran down the slope to where her aunt walked with slumping shoulders, her gaze on the ground, all unaware of the troops of fairies that filled the air around her.